'08

For Hunter,

Happy 3rd Birthday!

Love,
Grampa

Author Caroline Castle
Editor Clare Weaver
Designer Alix Wood
Illustrator Daniel Howarth

Publisher Steve Evans
Creative Director Zeta Davies
Senior Editor Hannah Ray

Sandy Creek
122 Fifth Avenue
New York, NY 10011

ISBN 978 1 4351 0995 7

Library of Congress Control Number: 2006038438

Printed and bound in China

10 9 8 7 6 5 4 3 2 1

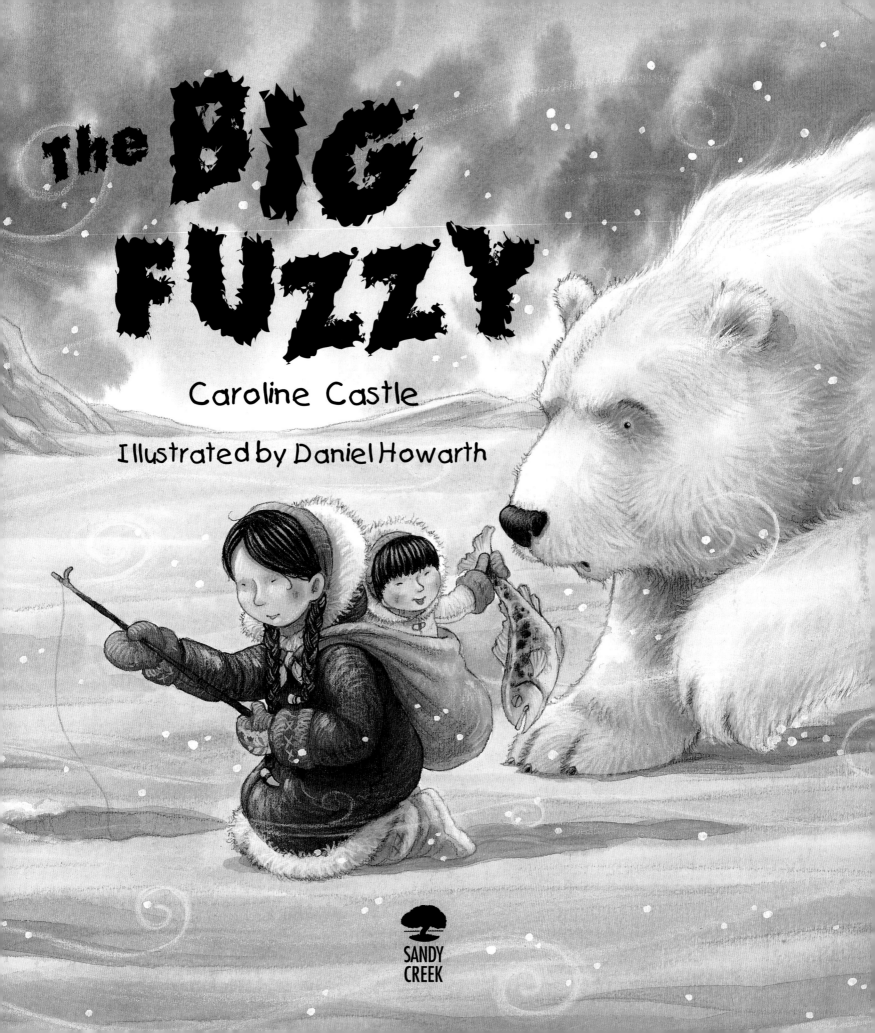

the BIG FUZZY

Caroline Castle

Illustrated by Daniel Howarth

SANDY CREEK

This is a story that happened long ago in a
faraway land covered in snow. The land was
called Greenland and still is today.

One **cold**, **cold** morning,

a domed shape rose out of the mist.

It was a little house made of ice! An **IGLOO**!

Someone was coming out the door.
It was Little Sira with her baby brother
Ivik strapped to her back.

Little Sira's mother was sick and couldn't get out of bed. Sira had to go out to catch some fish for supper or the family would go hungry.

"Be safe, brave Little Sira," called her mom. "And watch out for polar bears."

But as they set off, someone saw them go. Someone big and **white** and **fearsome**.

Oh, it was so very cold. But Little Sira
was wrapped up warm as a winter fire.
She made her way slowly through
the snow until she came to
a good place to fish.

Little Sira dug a hole in the ice and sank her line and hook. The sun was bright in the sky, and baby Ivik was sleeping.

But someone was watching. Someone big and **white** and *fearsome*.

Very soon, Little Sira caught her first fish!

But someone big and **white** and **fearsome** was creeping up behind her.

Someone big and **white** and **fearsome**...
and **hungry**.

Baby Ivik woke up. "Big Fuzzy!" he laughed at the huge, furry face.

"Here," he said, "fishy?"

The big, white creature was so surprised that he took the fish and gobbled it up.

Little Sira caught another fish, and another.

"Fishies for Fuzzy!" laughed Ivik.

The big, furry creature gobbled them all up, bones and all.

The sky grew darker.
Little Sira heard the wind howl.
It whipped up the snow
and whistled around her ears.
She knew it would soon turn into a blizzard.
It was time to pack up the fish and go home.

But when she turned around, all
the fish were gone—every one!

"Naughty Ivik!"

cried Little Sira.
She was very cross.

But how could her little brother have eaten all those fish? He was much too small. Perhaps a seal came by and took them? Now there was nothing for the family to eat.

"Big Fuzzy,"

said Ivik.

Whoooo! Whoooo!
howled the wind.
The sky grew darker
still. Fish or no fish,
Little Sira knew they
must go at once,
while they could still
see the way home.

So, Little Sira and
baby Ivik set off into
the blustery evening.
But the wind roared
like thunder and
blew snow into their
faces. Sira couldn't
see the way.

Very soon,
Little Sira
and baby
Ivik were
both lost.

The nighttime fell like a thick, dark blanket.

And someone was following them. Someone **big** and **white** and

fearsome.

Little Sira saw the shadow of a huge creature behind her. "Oh, something is coming," she cried out.

"Something **huge** and **fearsome!**"

Little Sira ran as fast as she could, but the snow was thick and she was tired. Ivik felt heavy, like a big sack of potatoes tied to her back.

Soon, she found herself by an icy cave. "We can hide in here," she said. They were so tired that they fell asleep right away.

They didn't hear the big footsteps
thundering through the snow.
One, two, **three**...

Slowly, slowly, the big creature
crept inside. He opened up his
huge, strong arms, and...

...very carefully picked up Little Sira and Ivik and folded them into his warm chest.

Then he ran and ran as fast as he could, over the snowy hills and through the blustery blizzard, all the way back to the igloo.

Little Sira and baby Ivik woke
up in their doorway.

Little Sira couldn't believe her eyes.
How did they get home?

And where did that
big fish come from?

Only baby Ivik guessed
the answer. "Big Fuzzy,"
he said happily.